Written and designed by Sarah Phillips and Annie Simpson.

Oliver's Winter Adventure

Illustrated by Clare Fennell

make
believe
ideas

One fine winter morning Oliver awoke from a long sleep.

"It must be time to get up," he said to himself.

"Look how bright the light is!"

He put

on his

scarf,

picked up

his hat,

and

tiptoed

past

Mommy

Bear's

bed.

Oliver opened the door
and was dazzled by the
glittering glare.

The trees were wearing
white, fluffy coats
and the ground was as
cold as ice cream.

the Bear ResiDence

do Not Disturb

"This must
be snow!"

thought Oliver.

"How strange
it looks!

I'm going
exploring!"

As Oliver **set off** towards the trees, he sang to himself:

"I'm walking through the forest,

I'm a *big*, brave bear!

I'll climb a tree

and *see* what I *see*!

I'm not scared!"

From the top of the Big Pine,

Oliver gazed at the snow-clad forest,

sparkling like

a million crystals

in the sunshine.

The forest

looked different.

It even smelled different!

Oliver **jumped down** from the Big Pine.

He landed on his bottom and began to **slide.**

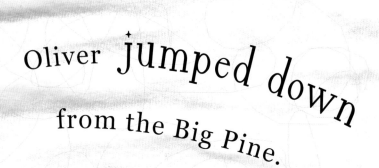

Wh**e**e**e**

He slipped down the slope, **faster** and **faster**, until **THUD,**

he hit a soft, white bank of snow.

"Wow!" he cried.

"That was amazing!

I'll do it again!"

And he climbed back up the slope, singing:

"I'm walking through the forest,

I'm a *big*, brave bear!

Watch me go

on the slippery snow!

I'm not scared!"

Sliding was fun,

but after a while,

Oliver began to feel lonely.

"I know," he said to himself.

"I'll make a Snow Bear friend."   So he got busy, pushing, piling, and

rolling the snow, singing as he worked:

"I'm walking through the forest, I'm a very brave bear!
I'll burrow and dig to build something big! I'm not scared!"

"HELLO!"

said Oliver

in his **biggest** voice.

But Snow Bear did not reply.

"What's all that **noise?**"

said a little voice

from the trees,

and with a

"tweet, tweet, tweet,"

Little Bird appeared.

"What a great Snow Bear!" said Little Bird.

"But he needs some hair. Wait here!"

Before Oliver
could say a word,
Little Bird flew off
and returned
with a mouthful of moss.
"Thank you, Little Bird!"
said Oliver.

"Snow Bear's perfect now . . .
but all that work has
made me hot!"

"Try this,"
said Little Bird, handing
him a spiky icicle.
"It's a real tweet!"

Little Bird and Oliver
licked icicles until they
were no longer thirsty.

"Thank you, Little Bird!" said Oliver.

"Would you like to come sliding with me?"

Taking Little Bird on his arm, Oliver sat down and

whoosh!

Down the slope they went, slipping, sliding, skidding, and spinning all the way to the stream.

"WOW!" shouted Oliver.

"TWEET!" cried Little Bird.

Oliver stepped onto the ice
and found that he could skate!

"Look at this!"

he called to Little Bird

as he spun round and round

and sang at the

top of his voice:

"I'm walking through the forest,
I'm a big, brave bear!
Watch me go
on the slippery snow!
I'm not scared!"

Oliver skated along the stream and onto the pond, twirling **round** and **round** in circles until . . .

THUMP, he fell on his bottom.

OUCH!

Oliver was upset. He felt **dizzy** and **cold** and **lost**.

Two **big tears** rolled down Oliver's face.

"Come on," said Little Bird.

"You're a **big, brave** bear, remember?"

Oliver looked at Little Bird. He couldn't manage a smile,

but he did start to sing very quietly:

"I'm walking through the forest,
I'm a *big, brave* bear!
To find the way back,
I'll follow my tracks!
I'm only a little scared!"

Slowly and carefully,
Oliver walked back **around** the pond,

along the stream, up the hill, and past Snow Bear,

singing
as he went:

"I've walked through the forest,

I'm a *big*, brave bear!

My home's in sight,

I can *see* the light!

I'm no longer scared!"

Mommy Bear was standing
at the door of the house.
"Where have you been, Oliver?
It's not time for us to get up.
It's much too cold.
Come inside this minute."

"Yes, Mommy," said Oliver.
"Bye-bye, Little Bird,
and thank you!"
"Tweet, tweet!" said Little Bird.

Mommy Bear gave Oliver a **hug** and **tucked** him into bed.

"We need another **long** sleep," she said.

"When we wake up, the snow will have **melted**

and it will be **spring**."

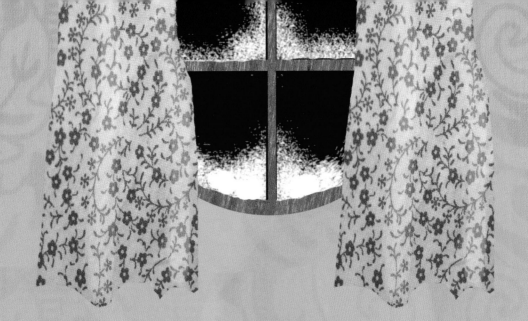

Oliver felt **tired** and **happy**.

He closed his eyes

and Mommy Bear sang:

"You've been walking through the forest,

you're such a big, brave bear!

I'll say good night, then you'll sleep tight,

until the spring is here!"

And before Mommy Bear could say another word,

Oliver was fast asleep.